Marissa
the Science
Fairy

To Sarah B, a true friend

Special thanks to Rachel Elliot

ISBN 978-0-545-85205-0

10 9 8 7 6 5 4 3 2 1   16 17 18 19 20

Printed in the U.S.A.   40
First edition, July 2016

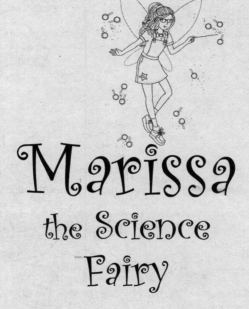

Marissa
the Science
Fairy

by Daisy Meadows

SCHOLASTIC INC.

The Fairyland Palace

Fairyland School

Tippington Town

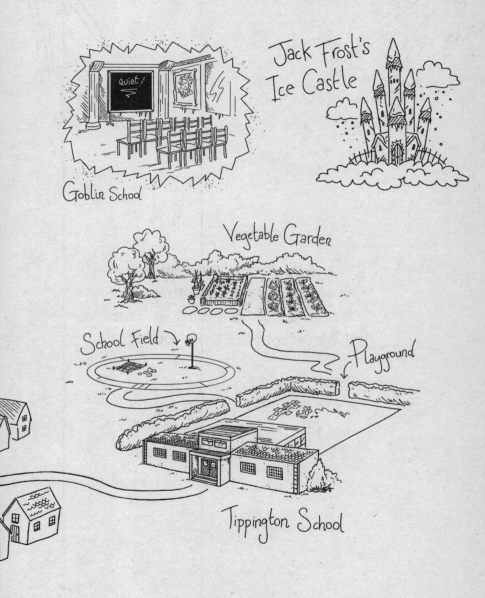

Goblin School

Jack Frost's Ice Castle

Vegetable Garden

School Field

Playground

Tippington School

It's time the School Day Fairies see
How wonderful a school should be—
A place where goblins must be bossed,
And learn about the great Jack Frost.

Now every fairy badge of gold
Makes goblins do as they are told.
Let silly fairies whine and wail.
My cleverness will never fail!

Contents

Best Friends at School!

Kirsty Tate smoothed down the jacket of her new school uniform and bit her lip.

"I feel excited one minute and nervous the next!" she said.

Her best friend, Rachel Walker, laughed and hugged her.

"Stop worrying," she said. "Just think how exciting it is that we are going to school together *for a whole week!* And you look really great in my spare uniform."

It was the first day of the new school year, and they were on their way to school. After weeks of late-summer storms and bad weather, Kirsty's school in Wetherbury had been flooded. It was going to take a week to get back to normal, and in the meantime her parents had agreed that she could stay with the Walkers. Best of all, she could go to Tippington School with Rachel!

"It's just a little scary going to a new school," said Kirsty.

"But you'll be with me in all the same classes," Rachel reminded her. "Besides,

we always have fun when we're
together, don't we?"

Rachel always knew
how to cheer her
best friend up.

"I have the best
times with you,"
Kirsty replied
with a laugh.
"We've had lots of fun

adventures with the fairies, haven't we?
Oh, Rachel, wouldn't it be amazing if
our fairy friends visited us at school?"

Ever since the girls had met on
Rainspell Island, they had kept the secret
of their friendship with the fairies. They
had often visited Fairyland together,
and the fairies had taken them on many
magical adventures in the human world.

"Look!" said Rachel, noticing three people waving at them from farther down the street. It was her friends Adam, Amina, and Ellie.

"Hi, Rachel!" they called. "Hi, Kirsty!"

Kirsty had met them on one of her visits, and when they smiled at her now, she instantly felt more comfortable.

"Did you move to Tippington?" Amina asked in an excited voice. "Ooh, I hope so!"

"Not exactly," said Kirsty with a laugh. "My school got flooded, so I'm staying with Rachel until it's fixed."

"Well, I hope it takes a long time," said Ellie with a grin.

"Me, too," said Rachel. Kirsty had a feeling that going to school with Rachel was going to be really fun! The first day back was always exciting, but because the girls were together, it felt extra special.

When they arrived at school, they sensed a real thrill in the air. Everyone was wearing carefully pressed uniforms and carrying brand-new bags. Shoes were shining, and hair was neatly combed. The school secretary was trying to keep everyone organized, but she was clearly frazzled.

"Ah, Rachel Walker!" she said, waving a clipboard in the air. "Is this your friend who is with us for a short time? Welcome, dear! Now, you are going to be in Mr. Beaker's class this year, and your classroom is number seven. Hurry along, girls, and don't be late!"

Adam, Amina, and Ellie were also going to be in Mr. Beaker's class. Together, they all went to the classroom. They were lucky to find a table for five at the side of the room, and they all sat down together. Kirsty had just taken out her new pencil case when the door opened and a tall, curly-haired man walked in carrying a briefcase. Everyone stopped chattering and sat up very straight. Kirsty and Rachel linked their little fingers. What kind of teacher was he? Would he be fair? Would he be strict?

"Good morning, class," he said in a friendly voice. "I am Mr. Beaker. Welcome to the start of a brand-new school year. I hope you're all looking forward to learning a lot and having fun this year."

He smiled, and his brown eyes twinkled.

"He seems nice," whispered Rachel.

Kirsty nodded, but she didn't risk whispering anything back. Mr. Beaker opened the attendance sheet and started calling out names to take attendance. He had just gotten to Kirsty's name when the door burst open and two boys leapfrogged into the classroom, giggling as they fell in a heap.

Mr. Beaker's smile disappeared.

"Boys, you're late," he said. "Stop

messing around and find a seat."

Kirsty nudged Rachel.

"That's odd," she said in a low voice. "Did you notice? They're in the wrong uniform."

The New Boys

The boys were wearing green blazers, and their green caps had extra-long brims that hid their faces. They swaggered to a couple of spare seats at the back of the classroom.

Mr. Beaker finished taking attendance, but the two late boys weren't on the list. He looked at them thoughtfully.

"I guess you're new to the school," he

said. "You'll have to get the Tippington
School uniform and take off those
caps. The students here don't wear
hats."

"But our green uniforms look much
better than the ugly Tippington colors,"
the first boy complained.

"We have notes that say we're allowed
to wear our hats," shouted the second
boy.

Rachel and Kirsty exchanged shocked glances. Neither of them had ever spoken to a teacher like that. Mr. Beaker didn't look very pleased, but at that moment the bell rang.

"Time for assembly," said Mr. Beaker. "Come on, everyone, let's go."

The class walked down the hallway in pairs, heading toward the assembly hall. Rachel and Kirsty were behind the two new boys, who were giggling and shoving each other. Everyone else was quiet, but the new boys didn't seem to care. The first boy elbowed his friend into the wall.

"Oops, sorry," he said with a cackle.

His friend shoved him back, giggling.

"Whoops, didn't mean it!" he said in a singsong voice.

The first boy held out his foot and tripped the second boy, who staggered sideways with a snort of laughter.

"Enjoy your trip?" asked the first boy.

Expecting the second boy to play the

same trick, Kirsty looked down at their feet. In shock, she nudged Rachel, who gasped. The boys had enormous feet, just like goblins!

"They can't be!" Rachel whispered. "What would goblins be doing at Tippington School?"

At the assembly, the children formed neat rows on the floor. Rachel and Kirsty sat next to the goblin boys, who were now playing tug-of-war with a pencil case.

"I still can't believe that goblins are in our class," Rachel said in Kirsty's ear. "Maybe they are just ordinary boys with really big feet."

Before Kirsty could reply, Miss Patel, the principal, stood up. Everyone stopped talking, and Miss Patel smiled.

"Welcome to a new school year," she said. "It's good to see lots of familiar faces as well as some new ones. This year, there are lots of exciting things to—"

Miss Patel broke off and stared at the new boys. They weren't paying any attention to her.

"I want to hold it!" the first boy was saying.

"Give it to me," whined the second, pulling the pencil case toward him.

"Boys, put that pencil case down and be quiet," said Miss Patel in a sharp voice. "You may be new, but I'm sure this behavior was not allowed in your old school. It's not a very good start."

The boys dropped the pencil case and folded their arms, sulking.

"Now, we need you *all* to be on your very best behavior this week," Miss Patel continued. "A school superintendent is visiting here in three days to see how well we are doing. Your teachers will be giving gold stars to any particularly good work you do, and it will be displayed for the superintendent. We want to show off your skills and talents, so let's all start the new year by trying really hard."

Kirsty and Rachel were so excited to hear about the gold stars that they stopped thinking about the big-footed boys. Then right after assembly, Mr. Beaker took the whole class outside to the school vegetable garden.

"We're going to start with a science lesson on plants," he said as they walked across the playground. "I want you to find specimens to bring back to the classroom. Then we will look at them under magnifying glasses. I saw lots of vegetables when I checked the garden this morning, so you will have plenty to choose from."

"I love science," said Amina, catching up with Rachel and Kirsty. "I hope I can get a gold star for this."

"I wonder who will get the first gold star in our class," said Kirsty.

Just then Mr. Beaker let out a surprised cry. The children at the front gasped.

"What's wrong?" asked Rachel, craning her neck to see over the heads of her classmates.

Someone had trampled all over the school vegetable garden! It was a total mess of drooping plants and squashed vegetables. Some of the plants had been pulled up and then replanted upside down, so their roots were sticking up in

the air. Everyone stared in shock at the awful scene.

"I can't believe it," said Mr. Beaker.

"Who could have done such a mean thing?" asked Adam.

Kirsty and Rachel had a very good idea about who was responsible. At the back of the group, the new boys were stifling giggles with bony hands. Then one of them grabbed the pencil case from the other, and they started squabbling again.

"They are definitely goblins," said Kirsty, catching a glimpse of a long nose.

"But what are they doing at Tippington School?" asked Rachel. "And why have they ruined our vegetable garden?"

A Trip to Fairyland

Mr. Beaker wanted to continue with the science lesson, so after the class had cleaned up the vegetable garden, they went back to the classroom. Rachel and Kirsty were given a dried-up bean to look at through their magnifying glass.

"Draw a picture of everything you can see through the magnifying glass," Mr. Beaker told the class.

Kirsty and Rachel peered at the shriveled bean through the glass.

"That's strange," said Kirsty. "It should look bigger through the magnifying glass, but it looks smaller!"

"Same here," said Ellie, who was trying to draw a squashed radish. "I can hardly see a thing."

"There's something wrong with the magnifying glasses," said Adam, giving his a shake.

"*They* don't seem to be having any trouble," said Amina, looking at the disguised goblins.

The first goblin was using his magnifying glass to look into the second goblin's ear.

"Yuck, it's all hairy and waxy!" he groaned, sticking out his tongue.

The other goblin grabbed the magnifying glass and peered up the first goblin's nose.

"Well this makes *your* nose look even bigger than usual," he said. "And it's full of boogers!"

"Keep the noise down, please," said Mr. Beaker.

The goblins paid no attention, and Kirsty frowned.

"Why is *their* magnifying glass the only one that's working properly?" she whispered.

"Amina, could you please water the plants on the windowsill?" asked Mr. Beaker. "They're all drooping."

Amina filled the watering can and carried it toward the plants, but water started to drip from the bottom. It was leaking! The

carpet was soaked, and so were Amina's shoes.

"Never mind," said Mr. Beaker. "We have an extra pair of shoes here, and I'll find a spare watering can at lunchtime. Now everyone take a ruler and measure one of the plants. We're going to keep a record of how much they grow this year, starting today."

Rachel and Kirsty thought that sounded like fun. They picked up their rulers and went to measure the plants.

"This can't be right," said Rachel. "My ruler says that this plant is four feet tall!"

"My ruler says that it's one-fourth of an inch tall," said Kirsty, examining the ruler. "Rachel, look! All the numbers are jumbled up!"

"Mine, too," said Rachel. "I can't measure anything with this."

All the rulers that Mr. Beaker had given out were the same. No one could measure the plants, and Mr. Beaker had to give up and move on to the next part of the lesson. He looked really disappointed.

"Rachel and Kirsty, could you please get the plastic plant pots from the cabinet outside the classroom?" he asked.

Feeling very sorry for their new teacher, the girls hurried out of the classroom.

"Poor Mr. Beaker," said Kirsty.

"Nothing seems to be going right for him today, does it?"

Rachel bent down to open the cabinet, and then tumbled backward as a tiny fairy fluttered out. She was wearing a cute denim dress and a purple T-shirt with an orange bow at the neck. Her long auburn hair was swept up in a half-ponytail, and she had a pair of cool, dark-rimmed glasses.

"Hello, girls!" she said. "I'm Marissa the Science Fairy, and I've come to ask for your help. There's a big problem at the fairy school. Will you come to Fairyland with me?"

"Right now?" asked Rachel.

Marissa nodded eagerly, and the girls grinned.

"We'd love to!" said Kirsty.

After a quick glance down the hall to check that no one was coming, Marissa made a figure-eight shape with her wand. Two golden rings of fairy dust

appeared in the air and gently landed
on the girls' heads like tiny tiaras.
Instantly, the school hallway disappeared
and they found themselves standing in
a rainbow-colored room. They had
been transformed into fairies, and
they unfurled their beautiful wings in
delight.

"Welcome to the Fairyland School,"
said a familiar voice behind them.

The girls whirled around and saw Carly the School Fairy smiling at them.

"It's fantastic to see you again, Carly," said Kirsty, hurrying to give her a hug.

They hadn't seen Carly in a while. She was standing with a small group of fairies whom the girls had never met.

Marissa took Rachel's hand and led her toward the other fairies.

"These are the other School Day Fairies," she said. "Alison the Art Fairy, Lydia the Reading Fairy, and Kathryn the Gym Fairy. We've all noticed that things are going wrong."

"What kind of things?" asked Kirsty.

"Well, in my science class, all the plants have died," said Marissa.

"The paint colors have gotten all mixed up in art class," said Alison. "Everything is a horrible sludgy brown color."

"The words have disappeared from all the books," said Lydia.

"And all the young fairies are flying backward in gym class," said Kathryn. "We really need your help."

A Disobedient Class

"I bet Jack Frost is behind all this," said Rachel, folding her arms.

The School Day Fairies nodded.

"He stole our magical gold star badges," Marissa explained. "We use them to make sure that all lessons are interesting and go smoothly. Without them, classes are a disaster!"

"Why did he take them?" asked Kirsty.

"He's using them to help set up his own school for goblins," said Carly.

"The worst thing of all is that Queen Titania and King Oberon are supposed to be visiting the fairy school in the next few days," said Marissa. "We wanted everything to be perfect, but without our magical star badges it will all go wrong."

"Let us help!" said Rachel. "We'll do everything we can to find your badges in time."

"That's just what I was hoping you'd say," said Marissa with a grin. "There's no time to lose. Jack Frost has set up his school inside the Ice Castle, and my magic can get us in there. Will you come?"

"Of course!" exclaimed Kirsty. "Let's go!"

"Good luck!" called Carly and the other fairies.

Marissa waved her wand, and there was a dazzling flash of golden fairy dust. When it cleared, Rachel and Kirsty were standing on a balcony overlooking a large hall. Marissa was beside them.

"We've been to the Ice Castle lots of times,

but I've never seen this hall before,"
Rachel whispered.

The hall was very grand, with pillars
of white marble and carvings of Jack
Frost on the walls. There were red velvet
curtains, and a portrait of Jack Frost
hung at one end of the room.

The hall was filled with uncomfortable-
looking wooden chairs, and on each
chair sat a goblin.

"Look at their clothes," said Kirsty in a
low voice.

The goblins were all wearing the
same green uniform as the new boys at
Tippington School. They were fidgeting,
pinching one another, and fighting.
None of them was paying any attention
to Jack Frost.

The Ice Lord was standing at the

front of the class, wearing a black robe and an old-fashioned professor's hat. He was trying to present a slideshow on the whiteboard, but he had to shout above the noise of the chattering goblins.

The first slide was a picture of Jack Frost wearing glasses. The caption said:

JACK FROST: FAMOUS SCIENTIST AND INVENTOR

"Jack Frost invented absolutely everything!" he yelled. "He is a genius. Write that down, you fools!"

Only one goblin, who was sitting in the very front row, started scribbling on a piece of paper. The others just crumpled up their papers and threw them at one another.

"Sit down and be quiet!" Jack Frost yelled.

"Come on," said Marissa. "He has no control over this class!"

She flew over the edge of the balcony

and swooped down to hover in front of
Jack Frost. Rachel and Kirsty were close
behind her.

"What are you
pesky fairies doing
in my classroom?"
Jack Frost
exclaimed.

"We're here
to take back
our magical
star badges,"
said Marissa in
a brave voice.
"They don't
belong to you."

The girls thought that
Jack Frost might try to catch them, but
he just sat down and folded his arms.

"Well, tough luck," he snapped. "I don't have them anymore. So you might as well just go away."

"Is that really the truth?" asked Rachel.

Marissa looked around at the unruly goblins.

"I think it *is* the truth," she said. "If he had the star badges, the class would be happy and well-behaved."

Just then, two of the goblins held a third one upside down and dipped his nose into an inkwell. Jack Frost bounded to his feet with a cry of rage.

"Stop that right now," he yelled, "or I'll expel you and send you to the human world, just like those other two mischief-makers. Then you'll be sorry!"

Kirsty and Rachel looked at each other, thinking exactly the same thing. He must be talking about the two goblins at Tippington School!

Quickly, Rachel whispered their idea to Marissa.

"Maybe they have one of the magical star badges," she suggested. "After all, their magnifying glasses were working when no one else's were."

"There's only one way to find out," said Marissa, raising her wand. "I'm taking us all back to your school—right now!"

Fairies in School

As usual when the girls visited Fairyland, time had stood still in the human world. They found themselves back in the hallway outside their classroom. Marissa had returned them to human size again, and she tucked herself into the pocket of Kirsty's skirt.

"Here are the plastic plant pots that Mr. Beaker asked us to get," said Rachel, peering into the cabinet.

When the girls returned to the classroom, Mr. Beaker was handing out some pods that he had picked from the garden that morning.

"Everyone take a plant pot and open a pod," he said. "I want you to take out the beans and plant them. There is soil on each table, and I have drawn the instructions on the board. Have fun!"

Rachel and Kirsty sat down at their table and opened their pods.

"Mine's empty," said Rachel, feeling disappointed.

"Mine, too," said Kirsty.

Almost everyone in the class had an empty bean pod. The goblins were the only ones who had found beans inside.

"Ha! we're way better at this than the rest of you," said the first goblin, sticking out his tongue.

Everyone watched as the goblins filled their plant pots with soil and then planted their beans.

"Very good," said Mr. Beaker as the goblins patted down the soil. "Now, over the next few weeks we will see tiny shoots begin to grow, and . . ."

Mr. Beaker stopped talking because something amazing was happening. Green stalks were already bursting out of the goblins' pots—poking through the soil, and growing thicker and taller in front of everyone's eyes.

"Impossible!" said Mr. Beaker.

"Magic," said Kirsty, as the beanstalks reached the ceiling.

"It's like something out of *Jack and the Beanstalk*," Adam exclaimed.

"Whatever they are, they can't stay in here," said Mr. Beaker. "Adam, go and ask the custodian to come get them and plant them in the vegetable garden."

As Adam hurried out of the room, Rachel leaned closer to Kirsty.

"This *must* mean that the goblins have Marissa's star badge," she said. "Only a science badge would make plants grow that fast!"

"We just have to find out where they're hiding it," said Kirsty. "Think, Rachel. Think really hard!"

Mr. Beaker walked around the room, placing a drooping plant on each table.

"I would like each of you to draw a picture of the plant and label the main parts," he said.

The girls opened their pencil cases, and suddenly Rachel froze. Then she turned to Kirsty, her eyes wide and sparkling.

"I think I know where the goblins hid the star badge!" she said. "Remember how they were fighting over the pencil case earlier? Each of them wanted to hold it. I think the star badge must be inside!"

"I'm sure you're right," said Kirsty. "Good thinking!"

Mr. Beaker was helping Amina, and he didn't notice the girls slip out of their seats and walk over to the goblins. The pencil case was lying on the table between them.

"Excuse me," asked Rachel, "could we borrow some colored pencils for our plant pictures?"

One of the goblins put his hand on the pencil case and pulled it closer to him.

"These are our pencils," he said rudely. "Use your own."

He pulled out a green pencil, and Marissa managed to peek into the case. Among the green pencils she saw a flash of gold.

"My star badge!" she whispered to the girls. "It's in there!"

Kirsty pulled Rachel behind the giant beanstalk, which had now filled the back of the room. All the other children were busy drawing, so no one saw where they had gone.

"We have to get that star badge back," said Kirsty, sounding very determined.

"Marissa, will you turn us into fairies again? Then maybe one of us can fly into the pencil case without the goblins seeing us."

With a wave of Marissa's wand, the girls were once again fluttering in the air beside her. The classroom looked very different now that they were so small, and their classmates seemed enormous!

Keeping out of sight, Marissa and the girls zoomed under tables and around chair legs until they reached the goblins. As quietly and slowly as they could, they peered over the tabletop. The pencil case was lying open directly in front of Rachel.

A Daring Plan

Rachel looked around. Every head was bent low over the drawing paper—no one was looking at her. It was now or never. She took a deep breath and swooped toward the pencil case. But just at that moment, one of the goblins looked up and saw her.

"Fairy!" he hissed, slamming his hand down on the pencil case. "Time to get out of here!"

He zipped it shut and climbed across the table, trying to reach the door. The other goblin followed him, and the fairies ducked under the table. They zoomed around the legs of their classmates, trying to stay out of sight and still keep up with the goblins' scampering feet.

Suddenly they heard a deep voice
shout, "STOP!"

It was Mr. Beaker, and he sounded
very angry. The goblins froze.

"How dare you climb onto the tables?"
exclaimed Mr. Beaker.

His voice was very loud now that the
girls were so small. He started to scold
the goblins, and the fairies hovered under
the table beside them.

"This is our last chance," Kirsty whispered. "Look."

She pointed up at the goblin who was holding the pencil case under the table.

Moving as quietly as they could, Rachel and Kirsty edged closer to the pencil case. They picked up the metal zipper and started to ease it open very slowly. The girls could only hope that the goblin wouldn't feel the movement until it was too late.

Marissa waited until the opening was big enough to fit through. Then she darted inside. Kirsty and Rachel held their breath and waited . . . and then the little fairy came zooming out with the star badge clutched in her hand. It had already shrunk back to fairy size.

"We've got it!" she said in an excited whisper. "Come on—back to the beanstalk!"

When they were safely behind the beanstalk again, a wave of Marissa's wand transformed Kirsty and Rachel back into humans.

"Thank you both for helping me today," she said, her badge back on her dress and her eyes brimming with happy tears. "Now the young fairies will be able to enjoy their science lessons again."

"It was our pleasure," said Kirsty, smiling.

"Tell the other School Day Fairies that we're ready to help them, too," said Rachel. "Good-bye, Marissa!"

The little fairy waved her hand and then disappeared in a puff of fairy dust. Kirsty peered out from behind the beanstalk.

"Mr. Beaker's still scolding the goblins," she said. "We can sneak back to our table now."

61

Mr. Beaker sent the goblins back to their table and told them to keep drawing. A few seconds later, when he looked around the room, Rachel and Kirsty were working on a plant picture together. It was as if they had never left their seats.

At the end of the lesson, Mr. Beaker came to look at the girls' work. They had labeled the root, stem, and leaves as well as several other parts of the plant. Kirsty had added a colorful rainbow over the top.

"This is excellent, Rachel and Kirsty!" said Mr. Beaker. "This deserves a gold star. I'm going to include it in the special display for the school superintendent."

Amina and Ellie smiled at the girls to congratulate them, but the goblins were jealous.

"What about ours?" they demanded. "Ours is the best!"

They held up their picture, but it just looked like a green scribble.

"Well, at least you tried your best," said Mr. Beaker.

The first goblin shoved the second one so hard that he almost fell off his chair.

"Where's the magic badge?" the girls heard him hiss. "You lost it!"

"*You* lost it!" snapped the other.

While they were arguing, there was a knock on the classroom door, and the custodian walked in.

"Where are these giant plants?" he asked.

Mr. Beaker turned to point at the beanstalks and found that they had both shrunk to the size of a small potted plant. His mouth fell open.

"But . . . but . . . they were huge!" he exclaimed.

The custodian looked doubtful, but then all the children started to speak at once.

"They were enormous!"

"They filled up half the room!"

"They were like trees!"

The custodian laughed and shook his head.

"Well, there's only one explanation," he said. "They must have been *magic* beanstalks!"

He walked out, still shaking his head, as Rachel and Kirsty shared a secret smile. The custodian had no idea that he was absolutely right!

"I wonder if there will be more fairy magic waiting for us tomorrow," said Rachel, as they cleaned up and put away their pencil cases.

"I hope so," said Kirsty. "There are still three more star badges to find . . . and I'm really looking forward to meeting the other School Day Fairies very soon!"

RAINBOW magic™

THE SCHOOL DAY FAIRIES

Rachel and Kirsty found Marissa's
missing magic badge. Now it's
time for them to help

Alison
the Art Fairy!

Join their next adventure in this
special sneak peek . . .

Puzzling Pictures

As soon as she spotted Kirsty and Rachel, the fairy did a happy twirl.

"Hello again!" she chimed in a singsong voice. "I'm so happy I found you!"

The fairy waved her wand with a flourish. A cloud of tiny artist's palettes instantly popped into the air around her. Each one was a perfect miniature, complete with brushes and ovals of brightly colored paint.

"We met yesterday, didn't we?" asked Kirsty, remembering their trip to the Fairyland School.

"You're Alison," added Rachel, "Alison the Art Fairy!"

Alison giggled with pleasure. She really did look as pretty as a picture. Her sunny blond hair tumbled in waves around her shoulders, topped off with a dusty pink beret. She wore a bright, polka-dotted T-shirt with a slogan on it, jangly beads, and a maxi skirt in different shades of blue.

"It's tie-dyed," she said proudly when she noticed Kirsty and Rachel admiring her skirt. "I made it myself!"

The cheerful little fairy was full of

chatter until the messy chalk drawings on the ground caught her eye.

"Oh dear," she said forlornly. "You can probably guess why I'm here."

Kirsty glanced nervously over her shoulder, then knelt down next to Alison.

"Is it your gold star badge?" Kirsty whispered.

Alison nodded furiously.

"I really need to get it back. My magical badge makes sure that all art lessons are full of fun and go smoothly! Imagine a world without beautiful drawings, paintings, and sculptures! What a terrible, gloomy thought . . ."

With that, the fairy's voice trailed off. Rachel glimpsed the tiniest silver tear trickle down Alison's cheek.

"We'll put things right," she replied

kindly. "The goblins can't get away
with this!"

Kirsty took Rachel's hand, her face full
of determination.

"We'll find your badge in no time," she
promised.

Alison's face brightened at once. But
before she could say another word, a
group of children ran past.

RAINBOW magic™

Which Magical Fairies Have You Met?

- ☐ The Rainbow Fairies
- ☐ The Weather Fairies
- ☐ The Jewel Fairies
- ☐ The Pet Fairies
- ☐ The Dance Fairies
- ☐ The Music Fairies
- ☐ The Sports Fairies
- ☐ The Party Fairies
- ☐ The Ocean Fairies
- ☐ The Night Fairies
- ☐ The Magical Animal Fairies
- ☐ The Princess Fairies
- ☐ The Superstar Fairies
- ☐ The Fashion Fairies
- ☐ The Sugar & Spice Fairies
- ☐ The Earth Fairies
- ☐ The Magical Crafts Fairies
- ☐ The Baby Animal Rescue Fairies
- ☐ The Fairy Tale Fairies
- ☐ The School Day Fairies

■ SCHOLASTIC

Find all of your favorite fairy friends at
scholastic.com/rainbowmagic

RMFAIRY14

RAINBOW magic™

SPECIAL EDITION

Which Magical Fairies Have You Met?

- ❑ Joy the Summer Vacation Fairy
- ❑ Holly the Christmas Fairy
- ❑ Kylie the Carnival Fairy
- ❑ Stella the Star Fairy
- ❑ Shannon the Ocean Fairy
- ❑ Trixie the Halloween Fairy
- ❑ Gabriella the Snow Kingdom Fairy
- ❑ Juliet the Valentine Fairy
- ❑ Mia the Bridesmaid Fairy
- ❑ Flora the Dress-Up Fairy
- ❑ Paige the Christmas Play Fairy
- ❑ Emma the Easter Fairy
- ❑ Cara the Camp Fairy
- ❑ Destiny the Rock Star Fairy
- ❑ Belle the Birthday Fairy
- ❑ Olympia the Games Fairy

- ❑ Selena the Sleepover Fairy
- ❑ Cheryl the Christmas Tree Fairy
- ❑ Florence the Friendship Fairy
- ❑ Lindsay the Luck Fairy
- ❑ Brianna the Tooth Fairy
- ❑ Autumn the Falling Leaves Fairy
- ❑ Keira the Movie Star Fairy
- ❑ Addison the April Fool's Day Fairy
- ❑ Bailey the Babysitter Fairy
- ❑ Natalie the Christmas Stocking Fairy
- ❑ Lila and Myla the Twins Fairies
- ❑ Chelsea the Congratulations Fairy
- ❑ Carly the School Fairy
- ❑ Angelica the Angel Fairy
- ❑ Blossom the Flower Girl Fairy
- ❑ Skyler the Fireworks Fairy

3 stories in each one!

SCHOLASTIC

Find all of your favorite fairy friends at
scholastic.com/rainbowmagic

HIT entertainment

RMSPECIAL18